Tales from Himself!
(Jack Cogan 1878-1961)

Retold by son JOE COGAN

Copyright © 2018 Joe Cogan

All rights reserved.

ISBN: **9781731058768**

DEDICATION

To my family whose unlimited love, sacrifice and encouragement through dark dreary winters and adverse financial times stayed me.

CONTENTS

Acknowledgments	i
Prologue	3
Camping Woes	5
Old Country German	7
The Shootout	10
Strong Coffee	12
Johnny "Groucho Marx" Carson	13
The McFadden's	15
Smokey & the Bear	17
Bill Sebring	19
Billy Cogan & His Pipe	21
Jerry Paquette	23
The Mash	24
Ralph & the "Old Lady"	25
The Marksman	27
Barney & Bridget	30

The Helena Ditch	34
Teddy	36
Father Conway	39
Roadside Service	43
Groves	46
Lady's Man	48
Pigs & Snakes	49
Rigid	50
Five Cowboys	51
"Spiked" Steak	53
Jim Frame	55
Mystery of the Thin Cows	57
Trip to Taylor Park	59
The "Chandelier"	62
Dad's Fearless Mother	63
Friskey Brothers	66
Cat 'n Mouse	69
Turkey Shoot	70

Prison Riot	72
Derby Under the Tree & David Jardine	74
"Coppers" & Whangs	76
The Rustlers	79
Nora	82
Flim-Flam Man	83
Redmond	85
1917 Model-T Truck	87
Rose Thief	88
Two Beers	89
Buck & Gag	90
"The" Parade	92
Git 'er, Dave	93
The Watch	95
Spiteful Suzie	96
Believe It or Not	97

ACKNOWLEDGMENTS

My thanks to my sister in-law Garnet Kleber and my niece Carrie Kleber for translating my scribble into ENGLISH!

PROLOGUE

Today is April 12, 2012, the 51st anniversary of my dad's passing, so I think it is high time that I write down some of the stories that he told the family and me through his life. He told all those old stories many times and they were always the same, with no divergence in language or enunciation. Since I am the youngest of his children, at age 77, I think I should do this because the other children have not heard the stories as many times as I have. I cooked for him for a few years when Elizabeth, his wife, my mother, passed away and he had gone blind. He was as Irish as "PADDY'S PIG," with blue eyes, soft pink skin, a slight dowagers hump on his upper back, and an Irish brogue as thick as Dublin mud with St. Patrick's tracks wandering through. Also evident was a twinkle in his eye, and a wry sense of humor that would wrinkle the skin on a listener's ears.

May good fortune follow me in this endeavor because I was never a good student, and my English teacher, Mrs. Celia Poplin, told me that my English and sentence structure was atrocious, and she was going to cheat my grades higher just so she would not suffer the indignity of having me in her class next year! TOUCHE!

Camping Woes

Chris Nachtrieb was one of Jack's best friends, being somewhat near the same age. Chris had another friend, Bob Brooks. These two were drinking buddies and often got into problems together. They decided to go to South Park to hunt antelope. They loaded their camp gear on a completely gentle horse and hit the trail. When they got near Dry Lakes it was evening and they were about to make camp. The so-called "gentle" horse lost his mind and went bucking into the timber. The top bedroll snagged on a tree and ripped open. It was near dusk and they tracked the horse for half the night by the white feathers spread behind the departing horse. They could not find the horse, so spent an extremely uncomfortable night by a fire. If you have never spent a night beside a fire without a blanket you do not understand what the word uncomfortable means. You are hot on one side, cold on the other, or vice versa. Smoke burns your eyes, your nose and your mouth, with an errant spark occasionally settling on you somewhere. When they would awaken during the night Chris would tell Bob, "I'm sure glad it was your bedroll on top. My bedroll is safe and yours is torn to shreds."

When dawn came the horse returned to the other horses, but the saddle had slipped under the horse and slid back against the hind legs. WELL! Even a horse has to GO sometimes! He "went" in the saddle and the adjoining bedroll. That ended the hunt and they had to return home to get new bedrolls.

Old Country German

Charlie Igney was an old country German. His speech was quite broken and hard to understand, except for the cuss words! He was a blacksmith by trade and had worked for the mines around St. Elmo. He was unable to make a sentence without bad language.

Two convicts escaped from Buena Vista Correctional Facility, stole two horses and headed west. They were dressed in war surplus khakis. Charlie spotted them coming up the Chalk Creek road. He did not know they were convicts and, being a blacksmith, upbraided them for riding lame horses. He then dug out some used horseshoes, nailed them on the horses and sent the convicts on their way. Soon after, two guards appeared asking if he had seen two men in khaki clothes. He denied this with his usual expletives, but told them about those two crazy people with pink clothes. The guards did not know that Charlie was colorblind and continued their search until they met a neighbor who saw the two inmates headed west. The guards caught up with them and took them into custody. Charlie was telling a picnic group that we were with about the episode using all his lousy vocabulary, spitting and sputtering! Mrs. House, a straight laced schoolteacher who was with our group said, "Charlie! Why do you swear so?" Charlie replied, "By*^%$##@%&!!! ME NO SWEAR!!!"

Charlie was working for the McMurry-Fehling ranch when a bunch of gypsies showed up. The other workers gave them a wide berth, but Charlie hung around them. When he came in for dinner, he said what wonderful nice people the ladies were. He declared, "The ladies even hugged me!" The boss said, "Charlie, have you checked your purse?" Charlie felt of his pocket, looked rather stunned, and went on with dinner, trying not to let on that he had been robbed!

The Shootout

Two local men, Charlie Pearman and John Pledger, hated each other. Whenever they got boozed up, each would declare that someday they would meet away from civilization and the other guy would surely die, punctured by six lead slugs, and would provide the buzzards with food. Dad opined that they were both cattle thieves and each was jealous of the other's thieving success.

One day these two men were riding horseback down two adjacent arroyos, each not knowing that the other man was there. The arroyos merged into one, and suddenly these two lunatics were facing each other, one with a .45 Colt, the other with a .44 Walker-Colt. They both went for their guns and blazed away! Twelve shots there were!-- Six from each weapon! With rearing horses among stinking black powder smoke and much thunder, both weapons were empty!

The man with the Walker could not reload his muzzle loading weapon rapidly, so sneaked off the field of battle before the other could reload! THE WINNER? Neither! The score? OH, YES! There should be SOME SCORE in ANY CONTEST!--------- One man had a hole blown in his hat! The other man had a concho blown off his saddle! Both men had SEVERE powder burns due to their proximity to each other, but neither man nor their horses suffered a bullet wound. So much for marksmanship!

Strong Coffee

Johnny Carson worked at the Mary Murphy mine near Romley. He did not like strong coffee. The miners liked their coffee strong! Johnny complained to the cook again and again. The cook, a huge, buxom, foreign woman, got her fill of his complaining and the next time he complained, she replied, "Mr. Carson, if you please! When I makes coffee, I makes coffee! And when I makes water, I don't makes it in the coffee pot!"

Johnny "Groucho Marx" Carson

Johnny married a young lady by the name of Ella Williams and they opened a grocery store in Nathrop. Soon after, Johnny purchased an automobile. He already had a shed that was open in front and big enough to accommodate the car. When he brought the car home, he first drove it up and down the street in Nathrop for all to see! He then aimed the car into the shed. He could not remember how to stop, continuing through the back of the shed, smashing the back wall out, and circling around and entering the shed again, and stopping this time! This writer believes the "Keystone Kops" movies were copied from Johnny's escapade.

Some years later, Johnny was working on the new road from Nathrop to Hortense Hot Springs in early spring. The workers encountered many mosquitos and two of the workers died of sleeping sickness. One was Johnny Carson. Johnny was a rare character, and looked exactly like Groucho Marx.

The McFadden's

The McFadden couple from near Riverside were fighting, arguing, and generally making life miserable for each other. They were up in years and set in their ways. Finally, they decided the best thing to do was to get a divorce. They each engaged an attorney to represent them. They were scheduled to go before Judge Bailey, a stern old judge, who was never known to smile while on the bench. The proceedings went on and on and George Hartenstein, who was representing Mrs. McFadden, began to question Mrs. McFadden. He said, "Did your husband ever threaten you?"

In her high, nasal voice, she replied, "Oh yes, he did!"

"Well then, please tell the court exactly what your husband said to you."

She replied, "Well--he said he was going to get rid of me, and get himself a nice young chick like George Hartenstein did!"

Judge Bailey instantly called a recess, and scurried into his chamber. Do you really expect that he didn't laugh??

Smokey and the Bear

Smokey Bennet was an old man who lived three miles east of Nathrop. The reason he was named Smokey was because he cooked in a stone fireplace in his cabin. Also, he was called Smokey because he never washed his face. His real name was lost to time. One day he was getting firewood and his little companion dog spotted a hibernating bear in a hole. Smokey went home and got his muzzleloader gun. He had a cap and powder, but no bullet. He scrounged around and found one buckshot, but it would not work for a bullet, so he wrapped it with wax paper until it filled the barrel and might work as a bullet.

Smokey spoke in short sentences with UH! at the end of each sentence. So the following is as he told the story. "I went back to the bear-UH! When I looked in, the bear was asleep-UH! And I stuck the barrel in his AIRRR-UH! I pulled the trigger and the rifle fired- UH! The bear got up and walked away- UH! Wherever he is, I know he's daid- UH! Because I shot him right in the AIRRR-UH!!!"

Bill Sebring

Bill Sebring was the Cogan's neighbor. He was a big man who had lost one leg in the Civil War. Still he weighed over 300 pounds. Because of his size he needed a big horse-- much bigger than the average horse. Bill's stump was always sore and he could not use his wooden leg very much. One day he went west two miles to the base of Mount Princeton where he shot a big buck. He wanted to take the buck home to avoid two trips. He put the buck across the saddle and lashed it down. He then climbed on top of the buck, but that left his wooden leg extra! He then held the wooden leg over his shoulder, leaving one arm to guide the horse. He started across the open park toward home. He just got out of the timber when the Buena Vista to Hortense Springs Stage drove into view. Bill had heard of some new laws, licenses, and seasons, etc. He thought he might be illegal, so turned right toward a strip of timber. The stage stopped, so Bill stopped. The stage started to move on, so Bill turned toward home. The stage stopped again, so Bill turned toward the timber. The stage resumed travel, so Bill again turned toward home. The stage stopped again, and Bill turned toward the timber again. The stage went on out of sight, so Bill again headed for home. This time he made it across the open ground to his homestead. A few days later, both Buena Vista newspapers had short articles about a strange object being sighted on Maxwell Park by the passengers riding on the Hortense Stage. No one knew for sure what it was, but it was bigger than anything they knew about, and some thought it might be some sort of sailing ship because it tacked back and forth and was HUGE!

Billy Cogan & His Pipe

    Brother Bill learned to smoke a pipe at a young age. It was always in his mouth and constantly set fires around the ranch. With each pound of Old English Curve Cut tobacco he purchased a carton of sulfur tip matches. He smoked as much sulfur as he did tobacco! He also occasionally set the corrals afire until brother Jack refused to put out said fires and would only call Bill to put out his own fires!

    One day he went home early, didn't feel good, and laid on the couch to read his Zane Grey book. He lit his pipe and settled back to read. He went to sleep, and when he woke up, the couch was afire. He jumped up and grabbed a kettle of water and put out the fire. Now the mattress was wet, so he hauled the wet mattress to the bunk house, trading it for a dry one! He took the dry mattress home, installed it on the couch, and laid down to read again, lighting his pipe. He went to sleep and when he awoke the new mattress was on fire!

Many times the pipe knocked his teeth out of his dental plate, but he always blamed anything else rather than the pipe. If a gate slammed on his pipe, it was the gate's fault, if a calf bumped the pipe, it was the calf's fault that the pipe knocked the teeth out!

One day a neighbor was near our place on the road and sighted a woman, dressed in finery driving a buggy, approaching a gate. The neighbor, being very dirty, opted to hide rather than to open the gate. The lady got out of the buggy and approached the gate. She lifted the loop and recoiled, looking at her sleeve and declared, "DAMN BILLY COGAN AND HIS PIPE ANYHOW!!!" Billy had reamed his pipe stem out on the gate wire! She knew instantly who the culprit was!

Jerry Paquette

Dad's father, Jeremiah Cogan, had a grocery store in Nathrop. He extended credit to many neighbors. One day Jerry Paquette, a regular customer, came in with a friend. The friend wanted to run a bill and Jeremiah Cogan said no because he did not know him. Jerry Paquette said, "He is okay. I guarantee it." The friend turned out to be shady and Jeremiah went after Jerry Paquette to pay the bill. Paquette refused and Cogan took him to court. When the judge asked Paquette what he said to cause Cogan to allow the charge, Paquette repeated exactly what he had told Cogan, lost the case, and had to pay the bill. Cogan, mindful that the defendant could have easily won the case by lying, admired Jerry Paquette for the rest of his life.

The Mash

Jerry Paquette had a still, well hidden from the Sheriff's eyes. He also had a fine draft stallion and sold stud service to others around the Valley who wanted to raise their own draft horses.

One morning before daylight there was a knock on the door and it was the sheriff and two deputies. They said, "We've come to get your still." Jerry opined that they couldn't find any still, but when they finished looking they should come back to the house, and have pancakes and coffee. After much looking, they came back to the house saying they found no still. They proceeded with breakfast and said what a beautiful horse he had in the corral. He not only was built excellent for pulling, but was extremely shiny and healthy looking and they wondered what he fed the horse to keep him in such wonderful shape. Jerry replied ——"THE MASH!"

Ralph & the "Old Lady"

The Harrington family lived in South Park. Ralph was the man's name, and the wife was simply referred to as the old lady. One day Ralph and the hired man were building fence and the hired man observed that Ralph was driving a staple alongside the wire instead of astraddle of the wire. The hired man called Ralph's attention to the mistake. Ralph replied, "I have fought with that damn woman until I don't know which side of the fence I'm on!"

As time went on the couple got more forgetful and senile. The wife decided it was best to put Ralph in the asylum. They obtained transportation to Pueblo, Colorado where the asylum was located. When they arrived it was late evening and the asylum would not open again until morning. The old lady rented a room for the night in a hotel. She intended to have Ralph committed the next morning. During the night, the old lady went wandering around the hotel in her birthday suit.

When the sun came up in the morning, the old lady was on the inside of the asylum looking out and Ralph was on the outside looking in!

The Marksman

John Cogan became an excellent rifle shot as he grew up. I have a clipping from the Buena Vista Yesteryear column about a rapid-fire match held at the reformatory. His first place score was higher than 2nd place and 3rd place added together. His prowess with a rifle was well known, and he profited some at shooting matches in various places. In those days there was no such thing as frozen turkeys, chickens, or geese. When a person won a prize, it was a live animal of any species. This caused home problems for Jack when his brother and he bought a new Model-A Ford sedan. It was 1929 and their respective wives were very proud of the shiny new automobile. Jack drove the automobile to a shooting match and did wonderfully well, winning twenty-one head of various animals, including a sheep for the best five shot group of the day---off hand at 200 yards!

He loaded all 21 animals in the shiny new sedan and proceeded for home. By the time he got home, the sedan was a mess. He now had an enraged wife, as well as a sister-in-law who was equally enraged. –WELL– EVEN DUCKS, TURKEYS, GEESE, and a SHEEP have to GO SOMETIME!!!!

When I was a boy about 7 years old, Dad spotted a coyote on a hill across the river. He called for his rifle which my brother brought from the house. He stood in the offhand position, took aim, and squeezed the trigger. There was the expected loud report, and when I opened my eyes–the coyote fell dead. I knew it was an unusually long shot, and a good one. In year 2012 I asked a friend, who had a rangefinder, to measure the distance because I had no way of measuring across the depression where the river is. The distance turned out to be 375 yards. I puzzled over this because no man can compute the trajectory of the blunt 30-30 bullet at that range, but now I believe I know the answer: Dad probably had erected a target at that place 40 years earlier to see what the trajectory of his new rifle would be!

One odd aspect of his targetry was that he refused to use a telescopic sight, claiming that he could see the target as well with just iron tang sights.

Barney and Bridget

Barney McQuaid was an early settler in the Valley, his wife, an Irish lady, named Bridget. They homesteaded a farm of 160 acres on the east side of the Arkansas Valley. Barney worked with 3 other men to bring irrigation water to the flat ground east of the Arkansas River. Barney was a determined old cuss and dominated Bridget too much. He would wake up at night and want a "spot of tea." Poor Bridget would get out of bed, build a fire, and make a cup of tea for Barney. Talk about LOVE!

Bridget had a big white cat that she kept cleaned and brushed. She was SO proud of the cat! One day the hired hands were cleaning the bunkhouse. The cat appeared. The hands petted the cat and inserted the cat in one end of the stovepipe. The cat came out the other end of the stovepipe colored quite gray. They threaded the cat back through the stovepipe and the cat came through darker. This continued until the cat was fully black. After a while Bridget called her cat. It ran to her, and she did not understand that, indeed, it was her cat. She grabbed a broom and beat the cat until the surprised animal ran away. The poor cat didn't come back until it had licked itself clean and was white again!

The pair had a small family, among them a son named Tom. Tom did not take to farming and spent a lot of time at the saloons and raising hell around Buena Vista and Leadville. He spent many days in the cooler of both towns for drunk and disorderly. He was young and strong and finally took up with a man from South Park named MacMicken who had some money, but was too old to run a ranch. Tom and he got together and Tom watched the cattle. They were getting along quite well. The cattle, however, became quite skinny in the winters, and Tom, having been Southeast near Kiowa, Colorado, came back to South Park telling Mac about all the grass that was available at Kiowa. In the fall they rounded up all the cattle that they could find with the JP brand and drove them to Kiowa. The winter turned mean and a blizzard set in. They locked their horses in the soddy with them to provide body heat until the storm abated. They dug their way out of the soddy and the horses were able to find forage on the windswept prairie. There were no cattle in sight but the horsemen were locked between drifts of snow of great depth. They survived in terrible shape, but the cattle perished in the arroyos, covered and suffocated in the snow. Returning home, Tom asked MacMicken if he could purchase the remnants that had been missed in the fall roundup. MacMicken acquiesced and Tom got started ranching on his own. There were more surviving cattle in Park and Chaffee counties than either Tom or Mac realized, so Tom got an excellent deal!

The Helena Ditch

The Helena ditch that supplies water to the level farm ground on the east side of the Arkansas River has always been a problem. The wing dam that spans the Arkansas River is located in rapids below the confluence of Cottonwood Creek and the river. About 1910, four farmers, whose lands were irrigated from this ditch, were trying to save the wing dam. The river was high and raging. Water pouring over the dam cut the west side of the dam away, creating a whirlpool. The farmers took their teams of horses and were trying to fill the whirlpool. They made a basket of chains to hold the rocks available on the west side of the river and were pulling these rocks, one at a time, to the bank above the whirlpool. Barney McQuaid was driving a team of mules. He chained an unusually large rock behind his team. He drove the team, pulling the rock to the high ground above the river.

He got a little too close to the bank and the rock rolled, twisting the traces of the harness around the mules back legs, and the weight of the rolling rock pulled the mules into the whirlpool. The team disappeared in the maelstrom and were never sighted again. Neither the harnesses nor the chains were ever recovered. About 1970, I was visiting with the grandson of Barney McQuaid and I related the story to him. His name was Lawrence Welsh, and at that time he was about 70 years old. He told me that the story was exactly true, and that he was a small boy at that time, and was standing a safe distance away and witnessed the whole wreck. Barney McQuaid had taken Lawrence, his grandson, to watch the work that day and he witnessed the tragedy.

Teddy

It is well said, a man is only entitled to one "favorite horse" in a lifetime. Dad's favorite was "TEDDY," named for his favorite president, Theodore Roosevelt. Teddy was long legged, black, with a white star on his forehead. Teddy loved people and he was in his glory in harness or under saddle. Whenever anyone stepped into his corral with a bridle, Teddy would step forward, mouth open, to be bridled. Dad's friend, Chris Nachtrieb, was helping with ranch work and Dad said, "Catch that black (horse) over there!" Chris opened the gate----bridle in hand. Teddy ran toward him; mouth open wide! In an instant Chris was over the fence loudly scolding Dad, complaining, "That damn horse almost got me!" Then Teddy stuck his head over the fence, mouth open, to be bridled.

Dad would harness Teddy to the buggy and go to Buena Vista with his elderly mother sitting beside him. He would go into stores and leave Mother dozing in the buggy. Teddy would stay where Dad left him, but spent his time dancing in place, rearing on his hind legs, pawing the ground, shaking his head, and giving passersby a huge, toothy smile. Town folks would run into the store and declare, "That damned horse is going to run away and kill your Mother!" Dad would simply say, "I think not." The local children learned about Teddy and would stand, as a group, in front of Teddy---all smiling, with Teddy returning the smiles.

Dad purchased a huge gasoline engine and generator at the 13,000 foot level of Mount Princeton for $50.00. He then had to bring it down. The road, and even the trail, had been obliterated by rock slides. Each flywheel weighed more than 400 pounds. The engine body was even heavier. Our neighbors had skid horses that they loaned Dad, but they were clumsy, and Dad had to rescue each one in turn from the rockslides. Dad then tried Teddy. Teddy made Dad nervous with his antics, but the horse knew where his feet were at all times and danced his way through the whole job without any problem. Then Dad had the generator to make our first hydroelectric. It served us well for six decades. Dad sold the gas engine for $50.00.

Father Conway

Father Conway came to Buena Vista. He was born in Ireland, of strict Catholic parents. He was reared in a stalwart family, and as a young adult, entered the seminary. He spent considerable years in study and prayer. Ireland had a more than adequate number of priests, so his superiors decreed that he would be a pastor in America. He was sent by his bishop to the small town of Buena Vista, Colorado. There was already a church in Buena Vista, and a rectory. He was well received by the parishioners of the area, such as the Mahon's, the McQuaid's, the Paquette's, the Beauregard's, the O'Connor's, the McPhilmys, the Cogan's, and many others. However, he had led a sheltered life and was not educated in the rough-and-tumble Western ways. The people of Buena Vista were mostly careful living people, and moral in their ways.

Father Conway did well and was much

appreciated by all. But he had heard about a place some 35 miles to the north named Leadville. Father decided to go to Leadville, but was not acquainted with anyone in that town. He obtained passage on public transport. When he arrived, he decided the way to see the town was to walk up one street to the end, move over to the next and to walk down that one. He continued this routine and eventually came to a street that looked quite prosperous. He told Jack Cogan that he only started down the street when a beautiful lady in fancy dress, and smelling of perfume rushed out of a house and gave him a handful of money. He thanked her and proceeded down the street, whereupon other ladies came out to the street, gave him money and went back to their house. This continued to the end of the street. Father Conway had never witnessed anything like this, and he talked endlessly about those lovely ladies in fine clothing who were so generous to a man of the cloth. Jack had to take him in hand, and explain to him that those lovely ladies were the prostitutes, and probably were conscience stricken by their immoral, and ancient way of life. This donation probably salved their conscience somewhat for their improper way of life!

Father was lonely for family, and wrote to his parents in Ireland, asking if one of his sisters might join him and take care of the household. He had his oldest sister in mind, for she was an excellent cook and a good housekeeper. The parents, taking note of his loneliness, sent the younger sister, who was great company, but could neither cook nor housekeep. Shortly after she arrived, two men appeared at the door with a sack of freshly caught suckers[fish]. They thought the Irish housekeeper could surely use the fish for a meal. This sister, named Alice, observed that said fish were still alive!

She asked the donors advice on killing them, and they replied, "Put them in a pan of water and drown them!" She did so. "And they splashed water all over my kitchen floor! I beat them with the broom, and still they didn't die--so I fed them alive to the cats!!!!!"

Roadside Service

Dad and brother Bill were delivering beef to Leadville in a C-Cab Model-T Truck. As they were passing through a cut before Pine Creek, a man jumped in the road, a distance ahead, waving his arms and pointing nowhere in particular. Dad stopped the truck, whereupon the man waved both hands. Dad stayed stopped. The man then waved one arm in a circular fashion which Dad interpreted to mean, "Come this way." Dad started forward again a short distance and the man jumped up and down waving both hands over his head. Dad stopped again and BOOM!!! An explosion went off right beside the open truck, almost blowing the two men out the opposite door. Shaken and scared they sat where they were until the man ran up to them and explained——a rock had rolled off the bank making the road too narrow for two vehicles to pass, so the road maintenance man had placed a "plaster charge" of dynamite on the rock, seeking to shatter the rock into manageable pieces for removal. The man was alone so had no one to guard the other end of the cut and didn't think anyone would be coming up the road, so he lit the fuse, then did not know what to do when Dad's truck appeared. Neither man was injured except for their right ears, which did not work very good for several weeks.

    They delivered the beef to Leadville, and were going on to Grand Valley to visit relatives. The route was over Tennessee Pass, past Pando, and Redcliff, then over Battle Mountain and down the Eagle River and the Colorado. As they were going over Battle Mountain, a Model-T car met them. The road left only room for one vehicle. Jack and Bill wondered how they could pass. Four burly men got out of the car. They each grabbed a corner of the car and lifted it up the bank and Dad drove past.

The four men lifted the car back on the road, cranked the engine and proceeded on.

They visited their cousins, the Sullivan's, in Glenwood Springs. Mr. Sullivan came to America on a sailing ship, then came to Colorado on a steam train. He was Irish as Paddy's Pig and was well versed in superstition. He would ride on a train but refused to get in an automobile. It seems someone told him that automobiles ran because of a series of little explosions within the engine. His great fear was that something might go wrong and all those little explosions would go off at the same time, blowing everything to kingdom come. In his entire lifetime he never rode in an automobile! Those things were too dangerous!

Groves

A man by the last name of Groves had a farm in a meadow on the south side of Buena Vista. He had bought a new red shirt and when it got dirty, he washed it. He was hanging it on the clothesline to dry, and an Indian rode up on a pony. The Indian exclaimed, "PRETTY SHIRT! PRETTY SHIRT! ME SEE! ME SEE!" Groves, thinking the Indian wanted to look at the shirt closely held it up to the Indian. The Indian grabbed the shirt, whirled his pony around and disappeared into the distance at full speed!!!

There was a road across this meadow always known as Groves Lane. A young couple had walked out from town and were sitting under some trees. Chuck Nachtrieb was headed home from a saloon. An owl was sitting in a tree and said hoo and Chuck replied, "It's me—Chuck." The story goes on, as all stories about an owl and a drunk, but after a while Chuck tired of the conversation and said, "IT'S ME ! CHUCK N—A—C—T——OH, HELL! I can't remember it myself so how in hell do you think you could remember it???"

Lady's Man

Chris Nachtrieb was a young man and liked to take the young ladies from Buena Vista for buggy rides. However, the horse was well fed and consequently was quite gassy. Chuck decided to train the horse to not pass gas, so every time the horse farted he would pop the horse on the rump with the buggy whip. The procedure did not have the desired effect because the horse would fart, then knowing it was going to be whipped, would jump, let a real RIPPER! And STAMPEDE down the road!

Pigs & Snakes

The Sedalia Mine, two miles northeast of Salida, had a refining mill near the Rio Grande tracks. The company that owned the mine and mill decided to tear down the mill. When they pulled the floorboards up they discovered the space between the floor and the soil was full of rattlesnakes. No one wanted to enter this place but one man knew what to do. He went to the neighbor, named Joe Robesnick, and borrowed a herd of pigs. They dropped the pigs in the hole and the pigs ate the rattlesnakes, from either end, or starting at the middle. The snakes never had a chance. Their bites had no effect on the pigs who enjoyed the meal with GUSTO!

Rigid

There is a story that if a coyote is chased to exhaustion one day, that the next day he will be completely rigid, and unable to move. Chuck Nachtrieb III told me that is correct. They once had a pet coyote named Smokey, and Smokey would follow their horses long distances, and the next day Smokey was absolutely rigid. Two men could pick him up—one on each end and he was rigid as a board, not sagging in the middle. His eyes were fixed and he was catatonic, not responding to anyone or anything until evening. Possible?

Five Cowboys

Picture this: five cowboys, riding single file up the trail on Brown's Creek. On one side of the trail is a Ponderosa Pine, with a limb jutting out across the trail. The first rider reins his horse around the limb. The second rider ducks down under the offending limb. The third rider lifts the limb high enough to pass under the limb. The fourth rider grasps the limb, lifts it, and holds onto it. He holds it—and holds it until he cannot hold it anymore---his horse walking on! His grasp slips! The limb recoils violently, hitting the fifth man full in the face, knocking him off over the cantle and the horse's rump, jamming his spur under the rear lattigo into the horse's flank. The horse departs, slamming into number four horse whose rider is dismounting. Both horses depart the scene, bucking violently, their stirrups popping over their backs with each jump, heading for wherever! Rider four crawls back to number five lying prostrate on the ground, and exclaims, "My Gawd! If I hadn't held that limb it would 'a killed you!!!"

"Spiked" Steak

Jack's brother, Billy, and a friend were riding far from home. The weather was bitter cold, and they were cold! They came upon a cabin, knocked, and no one answered. They entered and found no one. However, there was a quarter of beef hanging in the cool corner. They were tired, cold, and hungry, so decided to cut off some steaks to eat. The meat was frozen hard so they couldn't cut it with a knife. However, they found a two-man crosscut wood saw. They tried to saw off a steak, but the frozen quarter resisted by skidding back and forth with the saw. They located some huge spike nails in the corner. They spiked the quarter to the table, and it worked! They sawed off two thick steaks, but had no frying pan nor grease. By this time the stove top was glowing red, so they set the steaks directly on the stove top. They agreed that neither of them had ever eaten better fare in their life! They always wondered what the cabin owners thought when they returned and found some steaks missing, and several spike nail holes in their table.

Jim Frame

Jim Frame was a forest ranger on the Cochetopa National Forest—now the San Isabel National Forest. He was a young man, recruited from the local populace to protect the forests of the county. He was tall, slender and handsome. He was a horseman and rode horses in his duties. However, he was not an accomplished roper, not having done ranch work.

One day while riding up Magee Gulch he spotted a cub bear. The bear was standing on his hind legs with his head turned downward in a hollow stump, apparently licking ants. Jim thought it would be fun to rope and tie this little cub, take him home, show him to his friends, and then return him where he got him and turn him loose. He rode his horse alongside the bear, and readied his rope, holding the loop above the bear. The bear kept moving gently as he consumed ants. Jim soon got tired of holding the lasso and decided to speak to the bear thinking that the sound would cause the bear to raise his head, and Jim would drop and tighten the loop. Jim said, "HEY!!!" The bear, startled, jumped up and said, "WOOOOF!!!" right in the horse's face! The horse sidestepped violently, leaving Jim lying where the bear had been. The bear was last seen rapidly leaving for THE FAR SIDE OF NOWHERE!!!

Mystery of the Thin Cows

Dad was riding near the Big Trout Creek Spring and observed two old, thin cows. It was cold and was snowing and there was no grass for those old cows to survive on. It was late in the day and he thought he could come up the next day and get them. When he returned the next day, he couldn't find said cows. He looked everywhere he could think of, but to no avail. He decided that they must have "winter-killed." The next spring he found both cows in good shape and each nursing a calf. He was immensely puzzled and asked all the neighbors if they knew who had fed both cows through the winter. He finally asked a man who worked at the quarry, 1/4 mile away. The man said, "Yes," he knew, "Them damn cows spent all winter eating the horse manure from the well fed horses at the quarry." Each day when the Teamsters led their horses to the spring to drink, the cows would precede them down the trail, get their drink, and precede them up the hill to the manure pile. Hence–no tracks!

Trip to Taylor Park

Dad and Chris Nachtrieb would make a trip to Taylor Park every summer to fish and bring back fish to our neighbors. They fished in the section of river that is now covered by the reservoir. Nobody else fished the area and there were no game laws to obey so they caught many fish. They brought wooden barrels to store the fish in. First, they put dry grass on the bottom of the barrel, followed by a layer of fish, then a layer of salt. The process was then repeated until the barrel was full. These fish would keep for ten days if kept cool, and were very edible.

One day Chris fell in the river and couldn't get out. He floundered and sank. One of his friends managed to grab him, unconscious and not visibly breathing. He dragged him ashore to a large log and draped him over the log, and pounded on his back with both fists. Presently, Chris began to breathe and eventually regained his composure. Chris told Dad that when he was drowning he felt at ease and could hear nice music being played, but being dragged across the rocks to shore, and being draped over the log, and then being pounded on was absolutely and purely HELL. Chris recovered quickly and joined in the fishing.

The river was big and brawling and felled a couple of other men in the party. One man came into camp thoroughly soaked and cold. His friends got him by the fire, removed his clothes, and proceeded to wring the water out of his long underwear. They twisted and twisted, and decided to wrap the legs and arms around two sticks. This produced more water and they twisted until no more water showed. They then untwisted until it seemed straight and then they found that they had long johns that were now four inches wide, and 15 feet long. The poor fellow then had to go without underwear, so was the "butt" of many comments! Another man fell in the river and came back drenched and cold. His friends now knew not to wring his underwear out, so they built a big fire and held the underwear in the flame for a few minutes. When they took it out of the fire, it was only dry in spots. So they returned it to the fire for a couple of minutes and when they took it out the rest of it was dry, however, the former dry spots had now burned so this friend had numerous holes in his long johns! After the barrels were full they headed for home. As they descended Tincup Pass they met Griff Morgan and friends ascending Tincup Pass, thoroughly inebriated, and whipping their team to greater efforts with their fishing poles!

The "Chandelier"

Dad's friend, Mrs. Welsh, was a friend of the Tabor's at Leadville. She related the following to my Dad:

A new church had been constructed in Leadville and was not finished inside. The minister went to H.A.W. Tabor and asked if he would buy a new chandelier for the church. Mr. Tabor asked how much it would cost, and agreed to pay for the chandelier. Mr. Tabor then proceeded to count out the money, and put 10 times the money it would cost for the chandelier on the table. The minister asked Mr. Tabor what the extra money was for. Mr. Tabor replied, "When the chandelier arrives, I want you to hire the best chandelier player in Colorado to play it!" I suspect that story was told many times about that wealthy philanthropist.

Dad's Fearless Mother

Dad's mother was a small woman and not afraid of anything. She once beat a badger to death with a shovel. No one in this valley would get close enough to do the same because badgers are such fierce fighters. She also had a few geese, and the Irish way of harvesting down was to pluck them alive, so every spring they could get a new crop of feathers. But grandma was getting old and Dad volunteered to help pluck the geese by holding them while grandma did the plucking. The work did not go well, with both participants being bitten and flogged. Grandma was now unhappy with the poor help so she grabbed the goose away from Dad, placed the goose's head in her left armpit, and grasped both wings in her left hand, immobilizing the goose while she plucked the down from the goose's underside, with no help from the incompetent son.

A young lady was coming to visit Dad and his mother. Dad thought he would pull a trick on the lady, so he removed a dead mouse from a trap, tied a thread to the mouse, and when the lady appeared and sat down, he started to pull the mouse across the floor. The lady screamed, and Dad's mother, knowing nothing about the trick, made one quick jump, landing on the mouse and squashing its entrails out upon the floor. She then said, "Sure now! And wasn't it nice of it to wait for me to kill it!"

The Cogan family owned one mirror which was located above the washbasin to make sure faces were well cleaned. However, the mirror dropped, breaking to bits. Brother Bill and Dad were going to Buena Vista so were instructed to buy a new mirror. They bought the cheapest one available. However, when the box was opened at home the mirror was badly wrinkled, distorting ones' image. Their unhappy Mother remarked, "AYE! AN IT T'WAS A FOINE PAIR OF BYES AS BOUGHT THIS KOIND OF MIRROR, AN THEY HAVING THEIR FACES WITH THEM!!!"

Friskey Brothers

Friskey Brothers——Otto, Ern, and Gus first lived with their parents at the base of Mount Princeton. As they grew up they went to work at the nearby mines. They also had a small herd of cattle. They grazed their cattle near home and in South Cottonwood. When the forest service started, they obtained a permit in those areas for 100 head, but they only had about 30 mother cows. Otto was the main cowboy of the family, and the large permit on paper gave them cover to butcher their own cattle as well as some belonging to neighbors. Otto got caught butchering the neighbors' cattle twice in one week. He was therefore sentenced by the court to a term in the Colorado State Prison at Canyon City. Dad visited him there, and Otto said, "Jack, I have butchered our cows, your cows, and some cows of about everyone's near home, but Jack, so help me God, those two I was convicted on were planted!" This left brothers Ern and Gus to watch the cattle. One day these two showed up with black eyes, swollen lips, torn clothes, and obviously in pain. This family had each mother cow named, and the two brothers had a tremendous fight over which cow was missing. Was it Macguffy? Or Macginty?—I guess we will never know!

These two brothers then purchased the Schwander's Ranch where the mountain stream reaches the plain. It was cheap because it was in horrible shape because of the unchecked flooding of Trout Creek. The sand had covered the rich garden spots and orchard. The water was now invading the house when Dad and Mom stopped in to visit. Gus and Ern were sitting in the kitchen. The stream was running in the east door and out the west door. The brothers were attired in rubber boots and were laughing because the ashes from the stove were falling through the rusted bottom of the stove, and they didn't have to carry the ashes outside and dump them. When the sand got too deep, the brothers had to move, so they evicted the chickens from the nearby chicken house, and moved in. They never even shoveled the floor clean! The sand also covered the privy until the door no longer worked. They chopped a hole in the roof, and the neighbors said they witnessed Friskey's perched on top of the building obviously using the chopped hole for a toilet seat. OUCH!!!

In later years, Ern died and Gus moved back to the original place and bought some more land. Gus told me that there used to be five*&^%$#@! families living nearby and now I own the whole*&^%$#@!

Cat 'n Mouse

A homesteader that Dad knew built a small shed to store his saddle and grain. However, the mice found the grain and were eating much of it, so he decided he needed some cats. He went to a neighbor's place, and sure enough, they had more cats than they needed. He got a big cat and a little cat. The cats were either inside or outside of the shed. He solved the problem by cutting two holes in the door about a foot above the ground. A big hole for the big cat, and a small hole for the small cat. However, the little cat used the big cat's access hole instead of its own. He told the little cat not to do that, but the little cat paid no attention, so he told Dad that he shot it! Dad never knew if he really did shoot the cat, or if the man was just trying to make a lame joke.

Turkey Shoot

One of the stories Dad was most proud of was about a turkey shoot. Nine people had paid their fee, and the bookkeeper had collected their money, but wanted one more. A little boy stepped up and said he would like to try. Entry after entry shot, and were scored. Then it came Dad's turn. He shot a near center bull's-eye, clearly earning the turkey. Then it was the little boy's turn to try to best the others. He came to Dad and asked him to take the shot in his place. Dad asked the other entries if they would allow him to try. They all said it would be okay, but told the boy that Dad likely had the turkey anyway. Dad then shot, and when the target was brought to the shooting line---the bullet hole was not only in the bullseye, but was centered perfectly in the bullseye, earning the little boy the turkey. Second place was a chicken, but since Dad had now bumped second place to third place, he felt obligated to give the chicken to number three. Dad didn't get that turkey or chicken but was well reimbursed by the smile on the kid's face.

Prison Riot

Tyler Wright told this story to this writer. The convicts at the reformatory started to riot, as prisoners often did. They grabbed the preacher's hat when he neared the bars, then took turns crapping in the hat, and then handed it back to the preacher through the bars. When he realized what they had done he dropped the hat. They continued the riot for many hours with no signs of stopping. Warden Capp called Dad asking him to stand guard duty for the night, but not to bring his horse because in case anyone escaped they didn't want them to get the horse. Dad took his rifle and walked the three miles to the reformatory. When Dad neared the stockade, the prisoners recognized his long barreled rifle and his telltale limp and someone hollered, "HEY! THAT'S THAT GODDAMN CRAZY JACK COGAN AND HE'LL SHOOT US ALL!" The word passed quickly, and the riot was over!

What the prisoners did not know was that Dad would not have shot anyone except in self-defense! His reputation as an excellent shot was well known by even the inmates. Many years later I happened on a "yesteryear" entry in THE BUENA VISTA REPUBLICAN telling of Dad's first place rapid fire score being higher than second place and third place scores added together!

Derby Under the Tree & David Jardine

About 1940, there were two strange characters in the Pine Creek area. The first was, "DERBY UNDER THE TREE." That was the only name anyone called him.

He walked each day to the Granite Post Office just in case he might have some important mail. He never got any, but he thought he just might! He lived under a fallen tree with a few boards to keep the weather out. Few knew where it was. On his frequent trips to the P.O. he would cross Washburn's yard diagonally. This didn't bother Washburn because it was only a weed patch. But, one year, Washburn spaded the lot and planted potatoes. Washburn asked Derby nicely to use the road, but Derby kept on, with his big feet tromping down the potato plants. Washburn then pointed a shotgun at Derby's ear and told him nicely that next time he would pull the trigger! That had the desired effect on subsequent trips!

The other odd character was DAVE JARDINE. There was a story that his wealthy family supported him, provided he stayed away. He had many dogs of every description and would invite visitors to a roast dog dinner. However, nobody ever partook of this menu, so no one ever learned if he did eat dogs or if he just had a very odd sense of humor! After some years, neighbors told the Sheriff they hadn't seen him for some time and when the Sheriff investigated he looked in the window and saw Dave dead on the floor. The poor dogs had eaten part of Dave as well as some other dogs. The Sheriff had to shoot the rest of the dogs to retrieve Dave's body!

"Coppers" & Whangs

Running irons were a tool used in the cattle business to brand cattle with whatever brand one wanted. A running iron consisted of a three inch copper ring, approximately 1/8 inch thick, which was heated to a red hot temperature in a fire. The second part of this was two live branches cut from a tree and inserted from both sides through the ring. Squeezing these two branch ends in one's hand enabled a person to "paint" any brand desired on a horse or cow. This caused much problem if the wrong brand was put on a calf, therefore running irons were outlawed. However, most ranchers carried running irons on their saddles anyway, and most people were trustworthy. Dad's brother Bill had three "coppers" hung on leather whangs behind the left stirrup. Bill was, "OH, SO PROUD," of those rings! One day a group of riders were traveling together to begin roundup. One rider kept Bill's attention, while another untied the whangs holding Bill's running irons to his saddle. He put the rings in his saddle bag out of sight. When they neared the campsite, someone said, "Bill, you lost your running irons!" Bill fingered his empty whangs and said, "No, I didn't losted them! Some S.O.B. stolded them!" Bill was now irate, and because he was well known as a brawler, none of the culprits wanted to give the running irons back, risking a punch in the nose. So it was decided to hide the rings until roundup reached the Salt Works Ranch south of Fairplay, where the rings were hung on a nail in the stable. Presumably, the running irons hung there until some lucky cowboy found them and kept them as his own! No one on roundup ever told Bill what had happened that day on the range! Over one hundred years later, an arrowhead hunter found a copper running iron with W C stamped on it about 2 miles east of the Saltwork's Ranch!!! BELIEVABLE????

The Rustlers

Three drinking buddies decided to rustle a calf, so when darkness fell, they went to Smith's Ranch, and using a spotlight, shot a calf in the head, killing it.

An old neighbor of Smith's, hearing the shot, got out of bed, called the county sheriff for support, and went to the crime scene armed with only a rusty paring knife and confronted the three. I'll call the culprits one, two, and three, to prevent embarrassment for any other folk with similar names.

The neighbor confronted the three culprits, who weren't very sober (or smart), and told them he had called the sheriff and they should stay right where they were until the sheriff arrived. Number one, wielding the rifle like a club, swung it at the old neighbor. The neighbor ducked. The club swung over his head and cold-cocked number three. Now numbers one and two made a run for freedom, leaving number three unconscious on the ground. Presently he started groaning in pain and awakened to find the neighbor astraddle his chest. The neighbor was carving scratches about his throat with said paring knife and admonishing him to tell on his now absent partners. When the sheriff arrived that's sure what he did! But, when the sheriff put him in jail, he repeated and repeated all of the offense, until the sheriff had a doctor dress the head wound and give him a shot to put him to sleep so the other inmates could get some sleep.

Next came the arrest of numbers one and two. All three were found guilty as charged and given jail time commensurate with their crimes.

However, the soft headed judge granted probation so that they would not suffer jail time.

The end of the story is that the culprits

got caught stealing again, so parole was violated and the three had to do hard time after all!

Nora

Dad's sister, Nora, worked as a cook for the railroad, so fed trainmen and laborers alike. One day she made cream puffs for a treat and put a bowl full on the table. One grizzled old guy took one, bit into it, cupped his hand over his mouth and ran out the door spitting. He then came back in very indignant and loudly proclaimed, "THEM DAMNED BISCUITS AIN'T COOKED!"

Flim-Flam Men

Jewish cattle buyers came to our ranch quite often and tried many schemes to flim flam the ranchers to get cattle as cheap as possible, and would then take them to Denver to sell. They sometimes worked in pairs or threes. One would come by and offer $25.00 for a steer. The rancher would refuse, saying it was worth more! The second man would come by and offer $10.00 for the same steer. Naturally, the rancher would refuse and tell him number one had offered $25.00, whereupon number two would declare, "I guess he didn't know that the market in Denver had dropped badly." Number one would then come back hoping the rancher was badly BLUFFED and try to buy it again for $25.00 - when the steer was probably worth $40.00.

One Jewish man Dad liked pretty well, that gave a pretty decent price, was Jack

Nunn. We heard he had got in a fight in the Denver Stockyards, cut his hand on the opponent's teeth, and got blood poisoning, which landed him in the hospital in Denver.

My Mother sent brothers, Jerry and Jack, to the store to purchase a get well card. They brought the card home and Mom read it. It declared, "SORRY YOU'RE SICK!

GET UP AND FIGHT!"

Mom sent them back to get a different card!

Redmond

Dad's cousin, Redmond Welch, came to the family ranch to live, but he had all kinds of schemes to avoid work. This became a burden on the workers in the family so he was requested to live somewhere else.

He went to a nearby town and pretended to be rich. He met a nice lady who also pretended to be rich - SO, they got married. The marriage failed as soon as they both learned that neither of them had any money.

Redmond left and went to Chicago where he bought a farm on payments. He had it surveyed and sold building lots. He advertised that the first baby born on one of his lots would have the money the parents paid for their lot refunded. The first baby born turned out to be TWINS! Redmond gave each twin an extra valuable corner lot! The newspapers told the story and the free advertising caught many people's fancy, and the lots sold like hot cakes. Redmond immediately did become wealthy for the rest of his life, just like he wanted: Without Working!

1917 Model-T Truck

Dad and brother Billy bought a Model-T, 1917 truck and brought it home, parking it in the yard below the house. They were talking about something else and when they looked around the truck was going faster and faster down the yard. Billy, who was used to stopping a team of horses by yelling "WHOA!," ran after the truck, now going too fast to catch, still yelling "WHOA, WHOA!" The truck didn't heed his command until it ran into the creek at the bottom of the hill. The truck was not damaged, so was pulled out of the muddy creek bottom by a team of HORSES - they knew what giddy up and whoa meant. Both brothers quickly learned how to use the hand brake and/or a block of wood to prevent the truck from moving.

Rose Thief

Brother Billy went to Salt Lake City to work and see his cousin Margaret Brennan - a young, gorgeous lady. As they walked down the street, they went by a large rose bush in full bloom. Margaret remarked, "I would like a bouquet of roses such as those!" Billy stopped, pulled out his folded pocket knife and proceed to cut those very roses she had admired. The lady who owned the roses stuck her head out the window and said, "WELL! COULD I FURNISH A SCISSORS TO HELP YOU STEAL MY ROSES?!!" Billy, never at a loss for words, replied, "NO, THANK YOU, MUM. I'm doing right well with my jackknife!" Margaret was mortified! Billy carried "his" bouquet of roses till they reached her house and she never walked downtown again with Billy!

Two Beers

Uncle Billy took my brother Jack to Salida while delivering beef. When the deal was finished, Billy went into a bar for a beer - ordered two tall ones, one for him and one for twelve year old Jack. Another patron saw the beer delivered and decided it was his business. He arose and said, "Sir, I don't believe you should give that child any beer." Whereupon Billy, 6 feet tall and two hundred pounds of hard muscle, arose and leaned down to the nosy man and said, "I ordered 2 beers, I did! The bar keep gave me 2 beers, he did! And it should make no difference to you if I pour one of them down this child or pour it on the floor!" The man meekly replied, "I guess not!"

Buck & Gag

Chris Nachtrieb and Bob Brooks were riding range and spotted 2 coyote pups. Bob roped one, and knowing how the coyotes killed Nachtrieb's sheep, killed it immediately. He went over to Chris, who had his on the end of a rope and said, "What are you going to do with the pup?" To which Chris replied, "Oh, I'm going to BUCK and GAG HIM - take him home, and tame him!" "Well, how you gonna to do that?" "Watch and learn," said Chris. With the rope end tied to the saddle horn and the other end around the pup's neck, Chris confused the pup with a stick, grabbed the scared pup by the tail, and proceeded to swing the pup like a jump rope. He forgot that instant diarrhea was the coyote's best defense. The coyote turned loose all over Chris with the stinking mess. Chris, now enraged, jumped on the coyote's head, killing him instantly. Bob said, "Well Chris - is that how you buck and gag them?" Chris replied, "Ptoo! Ptoo! That's how I bucked and gagged that $*#!!!"

"The" Parade

When my father Jack and my uncle Bill were working on the ranch, they would dress up in their Sunday best to ride in any parade in Buena Vista. Someone told them there would be a parade in Buena Vista on Saturday. They dressed in their finest and went up to town. They were later than they realized, but were given the last place in the parade. All went well until the parade doubled back, so all entrants could see all other entrants. The lead buggy in the parade sported a large sign stating that the people following the buggy support the Ku Klux Klan! Here were two Irish Catholic boys, in a KKK parade. They never, ever, rode in a parade again!

Git 'er, Dave

Tom McQuaid hired Dave Walker to be his foreman on his large ranch. The winter turned cold and the ranch hands quit, so Tom and Dave had to go far south to bring some cows home to the meadow where they would survive in better shape. Dave was new to the area and he said he kinda thought Tom let a cow stray out a sidehill. Tom said, "Git 'er, Dave!" Dave, riding a good horse, went after said cow with a vengeance! He did not know there was a sheet of ice under the snow! The horse went down with Dave aboard, and horse, rider, and cow slid down the hill and piled up at the bottom! Dave said, "You S.O.B.! If you ever do that to me again, I'll shoot you!"

The next winter, snow again - no ranch hands, so Tom and Dave go to the same pasture and headed toward the meadow. Dave told dad, "I watched that old S.O.B.

let a cow wander off at the same place. Tom said, 'Git 'er, Dave.'" Dave just looked at Tom like a mad dog and said, "Go git 'er yourself, you old S.O.B."

The Watch

Two old men in Buena Vista had one big gold watch between them. It was unknown if they knew how to tell time, but the watch was never anywhere near the correct time. They would walk to a street corner and one would loudly say, "What time is it?" The other would pull the watch from his pocket and they both would loudly proclaim, "Well, who'd a thought it was that time already!" Next block, watch in the other one's pocket, and same show! Nobody ever knew if they wanted to impress people that they could tell time or if they wanted to let people know that they had a gold watch. When other folks looked at the watch, it was never even near the right time!

Spiteful Suzie

Gus Friskey married for the first time when he was seventy years old. The couple never got along very well - still living in their own respective houses. Suzie got sick and died. When Gus went into Foreman's Garage for some repairs - Jake Foreman said, "I'm sorry you lost Suzie." Gus replied, "She was the orneriest old heifer I ever knew! I was going to divorce her, but she died! I think she just did it for spite!"

Believe It or Not

The foregoing stories I have related, I have retold as accurately as I was capable. The following story I will relate to the reader sounds too fantastic for me to believe. However, I will tell it, and leave it to your discretion. My father absolutely believed it and was somewhat unhappy with me for saying it sounded too fantastic to be true.

Bill Cantonwine was an early settler in this valley. He was born in 1849 and died in 1931. As a young man he became a teamster–freighter. He bought a big freight wagon and four draft horses, and hauled heavy freight from the Missouri River to the boomtown of Leadville. He was not a tall man, but was spectacularly muscled. He was diabetic from childhood but understood the pitfalls and necessities of the diabetic problem. He knew that too much sugar would wreck his health, so lived mainly on protein. He would buy a case of eggs—30 dozen. He had a huge frying pan, and each morning he would fry 3 dozen eggs. He then would eat one dozen for breakfast, one dozen for lunch, and one dozen for supper. When this was eaten up in 10 days he would purchase whatever else was available—mostly meat and some grains, but always a frying pan full of food for each day. He also knew that he must sweat profusely each day, so had a harness built so he could pull alongside the horses for exercise. People along the trail thought this crazy man was trying to help the horses, but he admitted that he didn't think it helped the horses at all but it provided him with exercise to help defeat the diabetes.

The massive team and wagon was the envy of everyone on the trail westward, however, the horses needed forage and water each day. He crossed the plains and was starting into the Colorado foothills when he discovered a small ungrazed meadow with water and ample grass. He stopped for the night and unhooked the tugs and reins from the lead team. This pair started grazing away from the wagon. Bill turned to the wheel horses and released their tugs and was dropping the wagon tongue when he heard a commotion. Bill, thinking one horse had started to roll, as horses often do when unharnessed, turned to correct the situation before the harness got tangled and was surprised to see a huge grizzly bear on the horse's shoulder with its mouth on the horse's neck. The collar and hames were also in the grizzly's mouth, preventing the grizzly's mouth from closing on the neck. Bill's flintlock was unloaded and lying in the wagon so was useless. Bill had just released the wheel horses' collars from the neck yoke—an oak sapling about 4 feet long and about the heft of 3 baseball bats. He slipped the lynchpin from this neck yoke and swung it at the bear, hoping to blind the bear, to do whatever damage he could. This yoke had a ringbolt in each end, and Bill was trying to hit the bear's eyes. He swung with all his might, hitting the grizzly squarely in the eyes. The bear relaxed, fell to the ground, kicked a few times and was still! Bill's horses were scattered and leaving the vicinity. Bill grabbed some oats and a nose bag and followed the gentlest horse until it came to him. He then mounted and caught the others which were heading for the Missouri River. He managed to get one team hitched to the wagon and got his horses and wagon a mile farther, where he hobbled the horses and let them quiet down for the night.

Bill loaded his flintlock and returned to the bear, but the rifle was not needed—the bear was dead. Bill looked farther and discovered that it was an old bear, in poor shape, with broken teeth. It smelled terrible, like perhaps it had been eating carrion. Bill always wondered if the bear had died of something like a heart attack or if his blow to the eye area had killed it.

Bill went back to his horses, who were not injured. He spent several days repairing harnesses and letting the horses graze to replenish their energy for the mountains ahead. Bill carried one well-worn grizzly canine tooth---the only one unbroken tooth in the grizzly's mouth for the rest of his life.

Bill lived here in this valley and farmed and worked for others for a living, but the diabetes got worse and his wonderful physique declined with age and he died at 81. His frame and spectacular muscles shriveled away, and my oldest sister, Amelia, who died in 2016 at about 98, remembered him as a tiny old dried up man.

FROM THE AUTHOR'S DAUGHTER

I am blessed to have firsthand accounts of Dad's stories. I often take this for granted and do not always put them to memory. So I am tremendously grateful to Dad, my Aunt Garnet and my cousin Carrie for compiling them and creating this book. Sadly, the book will not be able to capture the emotion, laughter and sometimes tears Dad put into telling them. For those of you who do not know Dad, he is a gentle giant (well, maybe not always), kind hearted and giving. He is also as colorful as the stories he tells. I am sure you will enjoy his stories as much as I do.

Made in the USA
Monee, IL
03 May 2026

49437705R00069